I Spy Books for All Ages:
I SPY: A BOOK OF PICTURE RIDDLES
I SPY CHRISTMAS
I SPY EXTREME CHALLENGER!
I SPY FANTASY
I SPY FUN HOUSE
I SPY GOLD CHALLENGER!
I SPY MYSTERY
I SPY SCHOOL DAYS
I SPY SPOOKY NIGHT
I SPY SUPER CHALLENGER!
I SPY TREASURE HUNT
I SPY ULTIMATE CHALLENGER!
I SPY YEAR-ROUND CHALLENGER!

Books for New Readers:
SCHOLASTIC READER LVL 1: I SPY A BALLOON
SCHOLASTIC READER LVL 1: I SPY A BUTTERFLY
SCHOLASTIC READER LVL 1: I SPY A CANDY CANE
SCHOLASTIC READER LVL 1: I SPY A DINOSAUR'S EYE
SCHOLASTIC READER LVL 1: I SPY A PENGUIN
SCHOLASTIC READER LVL 1: I SPY A PUMPKIN
SCHOLASTIC READER LVL 1: I SPY A SCARY MONSTER
SCHOLASTIC READER LVL 1: I SPY A SCHOOL BUS
SCHOLASTIC READER LVL 1: I SPY FUNNY TEETH
SCHOLASTIC READER LVL 1: I SPY LIGHTNING IN THE SKY
SCHOLASTIC READER LVL 1: I SPY SANTA CLAUS

And for the Youngest Child:
I SPY LITTLE ANIMALS
I SPY LITTLE BOOK
I SPY LITTLE BUNNIES
I SPY LITTLE CHRISTMAS
I SPY LITTLE LEARNING BOX
I SPY LITTLE LETTERS
I SPY LITTLE NUMBERS
I SPY LITTLE WHEELS

Also Available:
I SPY CHALLENGER FOR GAME BOY ADVANCE
I SPY JUNIOR: PUPPET PLAYHOUSE CD-ROM
I SPY JUNIOR CD-ROM
I SPY SCHOOL DAYS CD-ROM
I SPY SPOOKY MANSION CD-ROM
I SPY TREASURE HUNT CD-ROM

I SPY
MYSTERY

A BOOK OF
PICTURE
RIDDLES

Photographs by Walter Wick

Riddles by Jean Marzollo

Cartwheel
BOOKS ™

SCHOLASTIC INC.
New York Toronto London Auckland Sydney
Mexico City New Delhi Hong Kong Buenos Aires

For Elizabeth Page Wick

W.W.

For Act II and French Woods

J.M.

Book design by Carol Devine Carson

Acknowledgments

Heartfelt thanks to Grace Maccarone and Bernette Ford at Scholastic; Molly Friedrich at Aaron M. Priest Agency; and to Linda Cheverton-Wick, Kathy O'Donnell, Maria McGowan, Greg Clark, Sue Coe, and Tina Chaden.

Library of Congress Cataloging-in-Publication Data

Marzollo, Jean.
  I spy, mystery: a book of picture riddles/riddles by Jean Marzollo; photographs by Walter Wick.
     p.   cm.
  Cartwheel books.
  Summary: Rhyming verses ask readers to find hidden objects in the photographs.
  ISBN 0-590-46294-6
  1. Picture puzzles—Juvenile literature. [1. Picture puzzles.]
I. Wick, Walter, III. II. Title.
GV1507.P47M37 1993
793.73—dc20   92-40863
                                                   CIP
                                                   AC

ISBN-13: 978-0-590-46294-5
ISBN-10: 0-590-46294-6

40 39 38 37   7 8 9 10 11/0

Printed in Singapore   46

First Scholastic printing, October 1993

TABLE OF CONTENTS

Picture riddles fill this book;
Turn the pages! Take a look!

Use your mind, use your eye;
Be a detective—play I SPY!

I spy a hammer, a rabbit, a pail,
A whistle, a button, a horse on its tail;

A pencil, a penguin, a car that is blue—
What else should you find? The blocks give a clue.

I spy two combs, a man with a bat,
A birthday greeting, a party hat;

A prancing horse, a bow on a bed,
And then, there it is! A present in red.

I spy a dancer, a clothespin man,
The letters in PLAY, a chair, a fan;

A racket, a gate, a squiggly shoelace—
Now turn to find the monster's face.

I spy a coin, a carriage, a nest,
A spring, and the missing key to the chest;

Tea for two, a toaster with toast,
Backward BOATS, and the dollhouse ghost.

I spy a thimble, a straw hat, a saw,
Six musical frogs, a red lobster claw;

A spoon, a cage, a wedding cake man,
And proof that a cat knocked over the can.

I spy a yo-yo, a red roller skate,
A mouse, and the numbers one through eight;

A soccer ball, a piece of string,
A house, and the stolen diamond ring.

I spy a monkey, three coins, the word FOX,
Two fish, four airplanes, a domino box;

A calf, AUNT CORA, a block with a B,
And the puzzle piece missing from page 33.

I spy an anchor, a brown-speckled egg,

Twelve bird tracks, and a horse's leg;

A fishhook, a comb, an old pair of specs,
A butterfly—and the pirate's X!

I spy a frog, a dolphin, a horn,
A cake with a B, a fiddle, some corn;

Four-and-twenty blackbirds, three white kittens,
RUB-A-DUB-DUB, and six lost mittens.

I spy a bell, a bubble, a lamp,
A pig, a bee, the moon, a stamp;

A pinecone, a phone, a pair of gloves,
And the name of the boy whom Kristen loves.

I spy a cricket, three hats, and a boot,
Two clothespins, a broom, a basket of fruit;

A watering can, a box that is taped,
A trumpet, an egg, and the bird that escaped.

I spy GLITTERS, a rooster, a frog,
A fish bone, a clown, a little hot dog;

Four anchors, a racehorse, a sewing machine,
And the eye for the mask on page 17.

I spy four horses, a peanut, a plane,

Seven red stars, a colorful train;

A chick, a fork, a four-leaf clover,
And the sneak who's kicking the dominoes over.

EXTRA CREDIT RIDDLES

"Find Me" Riddle

I'm in every picture—and that is that;

I'm black and dainty; I am a _____.

Find the Pictures That Go with These Riddles:

I spy a starfish, a statue of a man,

A hook on a line, and a watering can.

I spy an iron, a swan, a pen,

A runner's shadow, and number ten.

I spy a bug, a snail, a spoon,

And the one who jumped clear over the moon.

I spy a basket, an apple with a bite,

A fish, a hen, and a little flashlight.

I spy three ducks, a hot dog, a flower,

And a flag that matches the one on the tower.

I spy a camel, a queen, four aces,
Three boats, a bear, and two bunny faces.

I spy a bee, a pencil, a broom,
A little blue bird, and a key in each room.

I spy a zebra, a football, a scale,
Seven small hearts, a horn, and a whale.

I spy a boot, a tiny white owl,
A rabbit, a car, and a little trowel.

I spy a cow, a tawny colt,
A safety pin, and a small red bolt.

I spy a fish, a king, a key,
A gumball machine, and a ship on the sea.

I spy a glove, a wagon, a cork,
Six craft sticks, and a little pitchfork.

I spy a pen, a pig, and a parrot,
Two brass tacks, and an orange carrot.

MORE MYSTERIES!

Mystery #1
The Mystery of the Charm Bracelet

This charm bracelet was taken apart, and its charms were scattered throughout the book. Be an *I Spy* detective and find them all. *Clue:* Each photograph contains one charm.

Mystery #2
The Mystery of the Heart-shaped Box

What was in this empty heart-shaped box? To solve the mystery, find the box when it was full. Then, find each of its treasures hidden throughout the book.

Write Your Own Mystery Riddles

There are many more hidden objects and many more possibilities for riddles in this book. Write some rhyming picture riddles yourself, and try them out with friends.

I Spy Mystery Birthday Riddle
in the Round

You'll need to give a careful look
All around this birthday book
To solve ten challenges—one per year;
When you're finished, give a cheer.

Happy 10th Birthday to I Spy Mystery!

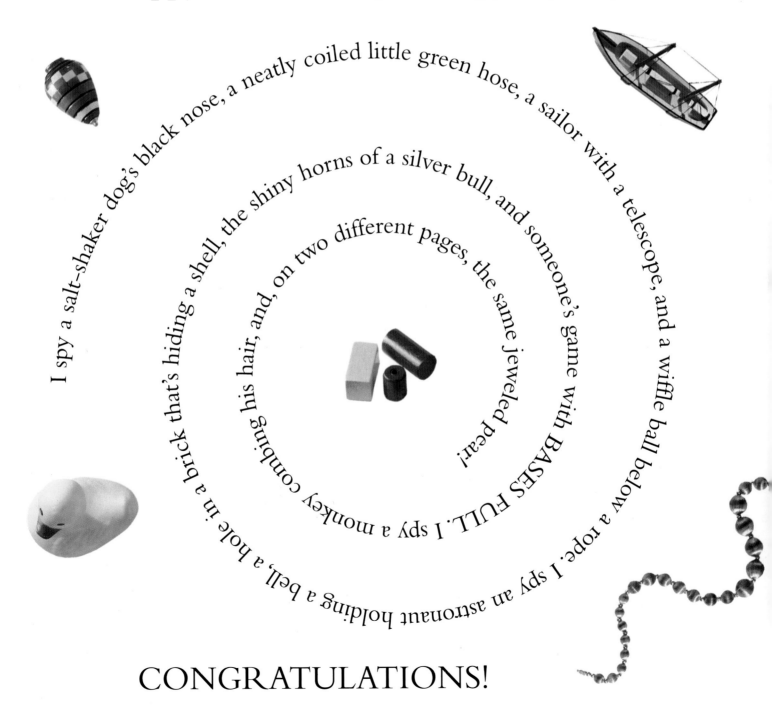

I spy a salt-shaker dog's black nose, a neatly coiled little green hose, a sailor with a telescope, and a wiffle ball below a rope. I spy an astronaut holding a bell, a hole in a brick that's hiding a shell, the shiny horns of a silver bull, and someone's game with BASES FULL. I spy a monkey combing his hair, and, on two different pages, the same jeweled pear!

CONGRATULATIONS!